ILLUSTRATED BY DAVID WIESNER

GONNA ROLL THE BONES

ADAPTED FROM A STORY
BY FRITZ LEIBER

ILLUSTRATED BY DAVID WIESNER

GONNA ROLL THE BONES

Story by Fritz Leiber,
Adapted by Sarah L. Thomson

MILK &
COOKIES
PRESS

New York

Distributed by Simon & Schuster, Inc.

Suddenly Joe Slattermill knew he had to get out of his house.

Around him, the old, decaying walls of wood and plaster were propped together, frail and unsteady as a house of cards. Only the big stone fireplace and ovens and chimney were heavy and solid.

Joe's wife baked bread to sell in those ovens. Over the years the heat and smoke had coated the mantle and the wall above it with a thick black layer of soot and grease.

Joe's mother knew, before he said anything, that he was going. Even
before he pulled his money from his pocket to count it, she shook her head
in disapproval. Mr. Guts, the tomcat, crouched near her, tail lashing,
hoping for scraps of the turkey she was eating. But she kept him away with

one hand. Joe's wife knew too, but she said nothing, only smiled at him over her shoulder. Joe shuffled toward the door. He said, "Guess I'll roll the bones tonight." No one answered him.

Hunching his shoulders, Joe set off down the dirt road that led past the cemetery to Night Town. The breezes were gentle but restless. They rustled the scraggly trees and seemed like ghosts uncertain whom and where to haunt.

Far in the distance, Joe could see a faint glow of gas flares and blue lights and neon pink tubes, all jeering at the stars where the spaceships flew. Night Town. He could hear a distant music, too, that grew louder as he walked along.

At last Joe stood before a three-story building. Above the doorway, golden light scrawled over and over, "The Boneyard," while a glaring red printed out, "Gambling."

So this was the new place everybody had been talking about, Joe thought. Open at last! He felt a stirring of excitement inside him.

Gonna roll the bones, he thought.

He dusted off his work clothes and slapped his pockets to hear his money clink. Then he threw back his shoulders and pushed through the swinging doors.

Inside, The Boneyard seemed as big as a town, and the bar looked as long as the railroad tracks. Joe heard the calls of the dealers and the slap of the falling cards as he coolly looked the place over.

Finally, Joe's gaze settled on the crap table. There he saw a man dressed in a long black coat with the collar turned up and a hat pulled down low, so that

only a triangle of white face showed. And at one end of the table was the fattest man Joe had ever seen, with a long cigar and a silver vest and a gold tie clasp that said in thick script, "Mr. Bones."

There was one empty space at the table. Joe traded all his money for chips and slipped into the gap. Then he lifted his eyes and looked at the man he'd seen as he stood in the doorway.

All Joe could see of the man's face was the smooth white forehead and the gaunt cheeks. The eyes were most impressive, sunk so deep you could hardly be sure you were getting a glimpse of them. They were like black holes.

And Joe knew his suspicions were right.

  This must be one of the really big gamblers, the kind who came to Night Town only once every ten years or so. This was the kind of man Joe had always wanted to try his skill against. He felt the power begin to tingle in his fingers, just a little.

Joe lowered his gaze to the crap table. It was almost as wide as a man is tall, covered with black felt that seemed to be sprinkled with tiny diamonds. As Joe looked, he got the crazy idea that the table was a hole all the way down through the world and the diamonds were the stars on the other side.

Then it was Joe's turn with the dice.

Strange, thought Joe. The spots on the dice were red, not black. But there was no time to think about it. Joe said quietly, "Rolling a dollar."

There was a hiss of indignation. The face of Mr. Bones grew purple as he started forward to summon the bouncers. No one at this table would dare place a bet so small.

But the Big Gambler raised his hand. Instantly, Mr. Bones froze. In a whispery voice, the Big Gambler said, "Cover the bet."

Joe picked up the ruby-spotted dice.

Now, ever since he had been a boy, when he'd won all the marbles in town, Joe Slattermill had always been incredibly good at throwing. He made a swift low roll, which ended up just as he'd planned—a four and a three. A seven. Joe had won his dollar. "Rolling two dollars," said Joe.

The next time, for variety, he rolled a five and a six—an eleven. Another win.

Nine throws later, Joe had over four thousand dollars. He knew that tonight he could win all the money at the table, but if he did, he would never get to see the Big Gambler play. And that was something he wanted to see.

"Betting a dollar," he announced, and threw the dice. As he'd known they would, they came up boxcars—double sixes—and Joe had lost his throw.

The dice went rapidly around the table, nobody winning or losing big, until they reached the Big Gambler. He held the dice for a long moment and then threw them towards the far end of the table.

The dice flew through the air without turning over, struck the wall at the far end of the table, and stopped there dead, each touching the wall along one flat side. A seven.

Joe was disappointed. What the Big Gambler was doing was ridiculously simple. Joe could have done it himself, of course. But he had never once thought of pulling such a trick at the crap table. It would destroy the beauty of the game.

And besides, someone might have questioned the throw. To be legal, both dice had to touch the wall. If they bounced off, everyone could see that they had touched. The way the Big Gambler threw, it was possible that one of the dice lay a hairsbreadth away from the wall or a bit lopsided against it.

However, nobody at the table objected. Besides, there hadn't been any of Joe's own money riding on this bet.

In a voice like the wind through the cemetery, the Big Gambler announced, "Betting ten thousand dollars." And he rolled another seven with exactly the same flat, stop-dead throw.

He bet another hundred thousand and did it again.

And again.

Joe was getting angry. It didn't seem right that the Big Gambler should be winning such huge bets with such machine-like rolls.

The Big Gambler kept on winning. Now he made the rolls without even glancing at the dice—watching, watching, watching Joe.

Just who, Joe kept asking himself, had he gotten into a game with tonight? But he didn't walk away from the table. He couldn't. Not until he got those dice back and could roll the bones again.

One by one, the other gamblers left the table. There was only the Big Gambler and Joe.

The Big Gambler whispered, "Rolling your pile."

It would take every cent Joe had to stay in the game.

The Big Gambler shot. Joe followed the throw with his eyes. Another seven.

"Satisfied?" the Big Gambler asked.

It was the biggest effort of Joe's life, but he swallowed and managed to say, "No. Lottie, the card test."

The dice girl let the card glide down the wall. After a moment, it slithered down behind the die Joe had suspected. That die had not touched the wall.

The Big Gambler bowed. "You have sharp eyes, sir. My apologies and . . . your dice."

"Rolling my pile," Joe said. Betting everything he had.

Then, giving in to curiosity and impulse, he cast the two dice straight at the Big Gambler's midnight eyes.

They went right through into the Big Gambler's skull and bounced around inside there, rattling. The Big Gambler spat them out into the center of the table. "Roll again," he said, as if nothing had happened.

Joe shook the dice slowly, getting over the shock. Even though he could now guess the Big Gambler's real name, he'd still give him a run for his money.

He decided to roll a seven, made up of a one and a six. The dice landed, rolled over, and lay still. Astonished, Joe realized that for the first time in his life he'd made a mistake. The six cube had come down okay, but the die that should have been an ace had taken an extra turn and come down six too. Joe had lost all the money he'd won.

"End of the game," boomed Mr. Bones.

The Big Gambler lifted a hand. "Not quite," he whispered. "Joe Slattermill, you still have something of value to me. . .your life."

Laughter burst out all over The Boneyard. Mr. Bones bellowed, "Now what use or value is there in the life of a man like Joe Slattermill? Not two cents!"

The Big Gambler raised his hand and all the laughter died.

"I have a use for it," the Big Gambler whispered. "Joe Slattermill, I will bet everything I've won tonight and the world and everything in it besides. You will wager your life and your soul. What's your pleasure?"

"It's a bet," Joe said.

He concentrated his mind as never before, the power tingled in his hand, and he made his throw.

The dice never hit the table. They went swooping down, then up,

and then came streaking back like tiny meteors toward the face of the Big Gambler, where they hung in his black eye sockets, each with the single red gleam of an ace showing.

Double ones. Snake eyes.

Joe had lost.

"Now," the Big Gambler whispered, nodding toward the crap table, "a bet's a bet. Time to take the Big Dive."

Joe put his right foot on the empty chip table, his left on the black rim, fell forward...and suddenly kicking off from the rim, launched himself in a spring straight across the crap table at the Big Gambler's throat.

The edge of his stiff palm caught Joe across the head...and the fingers or bones flew apart like puff paste. Joe's left hand went through the Big Gambler's chest as if there were nothing there but the black satin coat. His right hand, clawing at the skull, crushed it to pieces. The next instant, Joe was sprawled on the floor with some black clothes and brown fragments.

He was on his feet in a flash and he ran.

The whole population of The Boneyard was after him. Teeth and knives flashed. He was stabbed at, gouged, rabbit-punched, slugged, kneed, bitten, bearhugged, butted, beaten, and had his toes trampled.

But somehow none of the blows or grabs had much real force. It was like fighting ghosts. In the end it turned out that the whole population of The Boneyard, working together, had just a little more strength than Joe.

He felt himself being lifted by many hands and pitched out through the swinging doors so that he thudded down on his rear end on the sidewalk. Even that didn't hurt much.

He took a deep breath and felt himself over. He didn't seem to have suffered any serious damage. He stood up and looked around. The Boneyard was dark and silent as the grave. Joe saw a padlocked, sheet-iron door where the swinging ones had been.

Joe turned and headed straight for home, but he took the long way . . .

. . . around the world.

AUTHOR'S NOTE

I was a student at the Rhode Island School of Design when I first read Fritz Leiber's "Gonna Roll the Bones." I was captivated by the story, and I was excited by the imagery, which was so rich with detail and atmosphere.

My interest in wordless storytelling began to develop during my art school days, and for the last major project of my senior year I decided to attempt to create a wordless picture book. "Gonna Roll the Bones" was the story I chose to try to tell. This project was a great learning experience. It was the springboard for the wordless books that I would go on to create after graduation.

Turning my beloved project into a picture book required some rethinking of all the materials. Some of my original drawings were just too sketchy, and there were a few too many pictures of the main character walking down lonely moonlit roads. I created additional drawings to fill in some of the gaps, trying to retain the feel of the originals. Not an easy thing. Sarah L. Thomson artfully abridged the Fritz Leiber text to fit the picture book format.

This new version of "Gonna Roll the Bones" presents this Hugo and Nebula Award-winning story to a young audience, and takes me full circle to the beginnings of my book-making career. The illustrations were drawn entirely in pencil on vellum.

—David Wiesner

A publication of Milk and Cookies Press, a division of ibooks, inc.
Art © 2004 David Wiesner
"Gonna Roll The Bones" original story copyright 1967 Fritz Leiber

Distributed by Simon & Schuster, Inc.
1230 Avenue of the Americas, New York, NY 10020

ibooks, inc.
24 West 25th Street, 11th floor, New York, NY 10010

The ibooks, inc. World Wide Web Site address is:
http://www.ibooks.net

ISBN: 0-689-03591-8
First ibooks, inc. printing: September 2004
10 9 8 7 6 5 4 3 2
Editor — Dinah Dunn
Interior design by Brenden Hitt and Dan Taylor

Library of Congress Cataloging-in-Publication Data available

Manufactured in the U.S.A.

DATE DUE

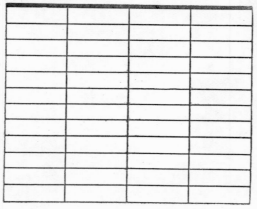

FRIENDS FREE LIBRARY
5418 Germantown Avenue
Philadelphia, PA 19144
215-951-2355

Each borrower is held responsible for all books
drawn on his card and for all fines on books kept
overtime — five cents a day on overdue adult
books and one cent a day on children's books.

DEMCO